You Decide What Happens

GOD ALLOWS U-TURNS

YOUTH

PASTRAMi Project

WRITTEN BY
Allison Bottke and **Heather Gemmen**

ILLUSTRATED BY **Gary Locke**

Faith Builder

Ages
9 and up

Wisdom

A Faith Builder can be found on page 90.

FaithKidz®
Equipping Kids for Life
An Imprint of Cook Communications Ministries • Colorado Springs, CO

www.cookcommunications.com/kidz

Faith Kidz® is an imprint of Cook Communications Ministries
Colorado Springs, Colorado 80918
Cook Communications, Paris, Ontario
Kingsway Communications, Eastbourne, England

PASTRAMI PROJECT
© 2004 by Heather Gemmen and Allison Bottke

First printing, 2004
Printed in the United States of America
1 2 3 4 5 6 7 8 9 10 Printing/Year 08 07 06 05 04

ISBN 0781439736

Designer: Granite Design

Collect them all!

To my newlywed children,
Kermit and Jennifer Bottke,
May your commitment remain as strong
fifty years from now as it is today.
I love you both.
−AGB

To Nick Pfifer,
You are a precious young man.
Your friendship with our family is
something we all treasure.
−HG

A special thanks goes to Vicki Caruana

who significantly helped shape this book.

[Love] is not rude, it is not self-seeking, it is not easily angered, it keeps no record of wrongs.
—*1 Corinthians 13:5*

This is a test!

You are the main character of this book. Your choices determine whether or not you are clapping in beat to your favorite band next to the cute new kid at your favorite concert or sulking by yourself at lunchtime.

Can you make it through middle school? Can you figure out how to handle friendships and faith, homework and home life without messing up? Better yet, can you make a U-turn when you do mess up?

Turn the page—if you dare.

PASTRAMI Project

"I'm open," you yell to Charlene.

Thunk. The ball is in your hands and you are under the basket.

"Shoot!" Charlene yells.

You shoot. You hold your breath as you watch the ball hit the faded backboard and bounce around the rusted rim.

"Yeah!" you yell as the ball drops through the broken chain-link basket. As you slap hands with your teammates, you decide there is nothing you would rather do than play ball at your old elementary school with your best friends on a mild Saturday afternoon. The sun is shining. You're making all

your shots. And Terry is playing. Terry! Your heart-throb. Life couldn't get much better than this.

But then the unspeakable happens.

"I've got to go do homework." Karen said it. Karen is always the one to ruin all the fun. She's one of your best friends and you just love her, but she still always ruins the fun.

"Yeah," says C. J. You knew he would. "Me, too. I'm outta here. See you guys later."

"You should go, too," Karen says to you. "It's almost 1:30. You're going to be kicking yourself on Monday if you don't go."

You know she's right.

"Aw, don't go," Terry says. "You can do homework tomorrow."

If you leave to do homework, go to page 11.

If you stay to play basketball, go to page 14.

"I'd better go," you say reluctantly. It's tough to pass by an opportunity to spend more time with Terry. You've been paying a lot of attention to each other ever since the concert you both went to. Today might be the day one of you works up to courage to talk about going together.

Terry leans against the fence and pretends to cry. You laugh.

"Sorry to be a heartbreaker, but I have homework to do. We're not all as brilliant as you are." Terry pulls off As without ever studying and relentlessly mocks the kids who do study.

"You can't do it tomorrow?" Terry asks.

"No. I told Mr. Mac I would drop by the school today. He's going to meet with a few of us who are struggling with his dumb science project."

"His class is so stupid. Why do we have to learn that stuff, anyway?"

"Beats me." You wave and start to walk away. "Anyway, I'll see you Monday."

"Wait!" Terry calls after you. "I'll come. I should probably get some brownie points from him anyway."

You can hardly believe it. Terry wants to do homework with you? Karen smiles knowingly, and you feel yourself blushing.

"Okay. Come on," you say. "It's almost 1:30."

As you and Terry walk toward the front entrance of the school, Terry leans in close to you as if to tell a secret. You wonder if this is it. *I'll say yes,* you think as you anticipate the question.

"Listen," Terry says. "Do you ever wonder how I can get As without slaving away at homework like you and your friends do?"

You slump a bit. This is not what you wanted to talk about. "You're just lucky, I guess."

"No. And it's not because I'm some kind of brainiac, either."

"Huh?"

"It's because I know how to find the information I need."

"What are you talking about?"

"What I'm saying is that there is an easier way to do homework. I know someone who's been collecting completed assignments and tests from kids who've graduated. He sells the stuff cheap."

"Terry!" you say.

"Do you want me to get some science stuff for you? Then we can play ball rather than sit in some rotten school on a Saturday."

If you say you'd rather do it the honest way, go to page 17.

If you like his plan, go to page 19.

Everyone but you and Terry leaves. You laugh, shoot balls, and flirt like crazy. You are so glad you stayed.

"I should be in school right now," you say when the two of you sit in the shade after playing for about an hour.

"Yeah, right," Terry says. "On a Saturday?"

"Yeah. Mr. Mac said he'd be there at 1:30 to explain the science project to anyone who doesn't get it."

"Bor-ing."

"Yeah. I can hardly believe I wanted to go."

"You did?"

"Well, my mom said she'll give me twenty-five bucks if I pull off an A on this project. She's even going to help me to do it. That's what we're going to do tonight."

"Cool."

"Cool. Except that I need to somehow explain to her what I'm supposed to be doing. I have no idea."

"I do. I can help."

"Really? Would you?"

"Of course. But listen, you don't need help from your mom."

"Why not?"

"Because I can get you completed assignments and even answers for tests for any subject by any teacher. It will cost you less than your mom will pay you for an A."

"You can get me a science project?"

"Definitely."

If you say you'd rather do it the honest way, go to page 54.

If you like his plan, go to page 19.

"You're crazy, Terry. I know I'd get caught some-how. Besides," you begin, feeling a little embar-rassed, "I guess I'd rather not cheat."

Terry shrugs. "Fine by me."

"How long have you been doing this?" you ask.

Terry looks away at something else and says, "Only since this year. Things got a lot tougher when we hit middle school."

You're quiet, not sure what to say next. You start walking further down the block toward the school.

Terry doesn't follow. When you turn around, you notice Terry is gone.

"So much for spending time together," you mum-ble as you enter the school.

"I almost gave up on you," Mr. Mac says as you walk through the classroom door. "Heads up!" he yells as a basketball flies straight for your head. You catch it without thinking.

"Good reflexes." He turns to the four other kids who showed up. "Now, let's see if we can get you guys to understand the difference between velocity and gravity," he says with a smile. "Once you get that, we'll go over the science project. Is it a deal?"

Mr. Mac isn't so bad. You never had a teacher who was so willing to make sure you knew what you were doing. You're still pretty shaken up by Terry's secret to getting good grades, and you're disappointed that you weren't spending the kind of quality time together that you hoped for. But as the afternoon draws to a close, you realize that you actually do understand the difference between velocity and gravity—and you are ready to explain to your mom how she can help you with your science project. Maybe this wasn't a waste of an afternoon after all.

"Heads up!" you yell and make a fast pass to Mr. Mac. Unfortunately he wasn't even close to being ready for it. The ball whizzed over his head and hit the floor before bouncing wildly in the corner by the trashcan.

"I guess you let gravity win this time," you say quite pleased with yourself.

"You could've taken my head off!" he says in that teacher voice you dread.

"I'm sorry, Mr. Mac. Really I am. I didn't mean to ..."

Go to page 80.

Just as school ends on Monday, Terry waves you over to the big elm tree. Terry is not alone. Billy is there too. *It's now or never*, you think.

"I want you to meet the solver of all homework problems," says Terry.

"Hey," Billy says with a grunt.

"Hey," you say.

"I'll leave you two to business," Terry says and strolls off in the other direction.

"Terry says you may be in need of my services," Billy says. "Normally I don't deal with someone I don't know, but if Terry says you're cool, then you're cool."

Terry thinks you're cool!

"I'm not sure I need your services. I'm just having trouble understanding my science project," you explain. Billy seems like a reasonable guy. Maybe this will work out alright.

"How much you got?" asks Billy.

"How much what?" you ask.

Billy gets impatient with you. "Money. How much money you got?"

"Nothing yet," you say.

"What do you mean *yet?*" asks Billy.

"My mom promised me $25 if I get a good grade on the project, so I thought I could pay you after I get that $25," you say.

"Doesn't work that way. You give me the money up front or no deal," he says.

There's only one way for you to get that money, but it means lying to your friends.

If you realize how wrong this is, go to page 64.

If you make a deal with him, go to page 65.

"No, I'm not the homework police. I'm your friend. Listen, why don't you let me help you with your homework so you don't have to cheat." You hope he will at least stop laughing.

"No way. I've got everything I need right here," Craig waves the black-market homework at you.

"Look, Craig, Mr. Mac made it so easy to understand today. Why don't we all get together at my house tonight and get a head start on our science projects?"

"You losers go ahead and waste your Saturday night. I paid good money for my project."

Craig sprints down the street, leaving you there to wonder.

Go to page 82

"You're such a loser," you say. "Cheating is for stupid people!" You've never spoken to Craig like this before—but you've never been this angry at him, either.

"You don't get it, do you?" Craig says. "You don't know what it's like to never understand the assignment."

"I still wouldn't cheat!" you yell.

"You think you're so perfect? Why don't you look in the mirror sometime?" he says and then stomps away towards home.

You walk home without looking back. Something inside hurts and your cheeks burn. Reluctant tears fill your eyes and you're afraid to blink because you know they'll start falling.

That night you lie awake replaying the conversation over and over again in your mind. You've known Craig since kindergarten. He may be difficult at times, but he'd never hurt you on purpose.

If you apologize to Craig, go to page 68.
If you don't apologize, go to page 70.

"Listen, guys," you say. "Mr. Mac made me realize that I could actually ace this class if I wanted to. And I figured if I could do it, we all could do it." You don't say anything about Craig, but you're thinking of him.

"What's wrong with getting Cs?" C. J. says. "Cs stand for *cool*, don't they?"

"Technically, Cs mean average," Karen says. "Personally, I think that cool should be way above average."

"Then maybe it's time we show what we're made of," you say. Suddenly you're excited at the prospect of being cool *and* getting great grades. What a concept!

"I'm in," Karen says and puts her hand up for a high five. "Who's with me?"

The four of you slap it high and down low.

"Well, four out of five ain't bad," you say. It was out of your mouth before you could stop it.

"Where is Craig anyway?" C. J. asks as he wanders back into the kitchen on the hunt for salty snacks.

"He had other plans," you say, being careful not to bad-mouth Craig in front of everyone else.

"What's more important than hanging with us?" Charlene asks. "We'll just see what he's up to," she says pulling out her cell phone.

"No, wait!" you say.

"Wait? Why?"

If you agree to call Craig, go to page 26.

If you don't want anything to do with Craig, go to page 28.

"So, what's the big deal about Craig?" asks C. J. "Why didn't he come tonight?"

"Because he's an idiot!" you blurt. And then it all comes pouring out. You tell them *everything*! Well, almost everything. The venting is focused completely on Craig. You conveniently leave out Terry. "He's so full of himself. He is willing to cheat just to make his life easier. I refuse to be friends with a person like that."

There. You said it. And it felt so good. But your friends are silent.

Finally Karen says, "You two have been friends since kindergarten. How can you just throw that away?"

You stare at her for a minute, shocked that she's not on your side. "I shouldn't have told you," you say.

"Maybe you shouldn't have," she says.

"I'm calling Craig," Charlene says, whipping out her cell phone.

"No, wait!" you say.

"Wait? Why?"

If you ask Karen what she means, go to page 71.

If you think your friends are being irrational, go to page 28.

"Uh, because I want to call him. Is that okay?"
Charlene hands the phone to you.

"Hi, is Craig home?" you ask, secretly hoping he isn't.

"No. And if I were you, I'd leave him alone for a while," says Craig's sister, Jenny.

"Why? What did I do?" you ask, beginning to get steamed. After all, he's the one who bought the homework.

"Craig's been walkin' around here all day saying you're such a downer," Jenny continues.

"I'm a downer? He's the one who isn't here right now," your voice gets too loud. Charlene, C. J., and Karen look your way.

"Well, he's not here anyway," Jenny says, obviously annoyed at you.

"Fine. I'll catch up with him later," you say and hang up the phone.

Just then you hear a *thump* at the living room window. You catch a glimpse of someone outside.

"What was that?" asks Charlene.

C. J. swings open the front door and says, "Boo!" to whoever it is.

"What are you trying to do, give me a heart attack, dude?" It's Craig.

"Hey man, where have you been? Get yourself in here," Charlene says. She pulls Craig in by his jacket sleeve.

You can't believe Craig had the nerve to spy on you.

If you ask Craig to stay and join you, go to page 30.

If you tell him to get lost, go to page 32.

"Because I don't want you to call that jerk from my house. You'll have to go home to do that."

You're surprised to see that your friends start packing up to leave. No one says a word. You feel lousy inside.

After school you see Craig unlocking his bike. He wasn't on the bus today, and now you know why—he's chosen an alternative mode of transportation.

"Hey, Craig, rode your bike to school today?" you ask and flash him your biggest smile.

"What do you care?" he snaps.

Craig doesn't seem interested in getting things back to normal.

"I just noticed, that's all," you say.

"Well, go notice somewhere else!" he says.

"Maybe I will!" you say.

"Do what you want. I'm leaving," he says. Craig peels off on his bike so fast the back tire spits dirt right into your face.

With grit in your teeth, you yell after him, "From now on, I will. Don't you worry!"

That night, for the first time in weeks, you are home alone. Days later you see C. J. riding with Craig, happy as can be. But Karen and Charlene avoid you both. Friendships are more than strained—they're broken. Five Alive becomes a distant memory that exists only in the yearbook photos.

The End.

"I just called your house. Glad you could make it," you say. You decide maybe you'll just put what happened this afternoon behind you.

"I was kind of hoping you guys would quit this new let's-be-serious-about-school routine and get back to more important stuff, like our chat room," Craig says.

This isn't going to be as easy as you thought it would.

"No way," Karen says. "We've got a plan."

Craig plops down on the couch next to C. J. and grabs a handful of sour cream and onion chips.

"I'm all ears," he says.

"Okay, well, it occurred to us that maybe we could improve our reputation a bit," began Karen.

"What's wrong with our rep?" Craig asks, shifting in his seat. He's now visibly uncomfortable.

"Dude, did you know Cs don't stand for cool?" C. J. asks with food in his mouth.

Sometimes you wonder if the only thing between C. J.'s ears is junk food!

"We know we're cool," says Charlene. "We just thought of a way to be even cooler."

The four of you talk at once and Craig follows the conversation with his head like he's watching a tennis match.

"Cool it! I get it. I get it already," he says holding up his hands for them to stop.

"What do you get?" you ask.

Craig reaches into his backpack and pulls out a handful of papers. What is he up to? You know you'll freak if he tries to convince Five Alive that there's an easier way—more expensive, but easier—to improve their reps.

"I get that I don't need these," he says.

You watch as Craig crumples the bought homework and tosses it in the trash.

"I don't know what I was thinking," he says turning to you. "I just blew $20."

If you forgive him, go to page 34.

If you don't forgive him, go to page 40.

If you secretly pull the homework out of the trash after everyone leaves, go to page 78.

"What do you want? And why were you spying on us?" you say. You are furious.

"He wasn't spying," Charlene says. "He belongs here, remember?"

"Not anymore he doesn't," you say. "I don't hang out with cheaters."

Everyone is stunned into silence. You didn't plan on spilling that news like that. Just a few minutes ago you were calling him to invite him over. Somehow when you saw him you got mad all over again.

"No way," Craig says. "I came over to work with you guys, that's all."

"You probably came here to steal our ideas," you say. "After all, that's what you're good at."

C. J. stops his munching and stands between the two of you. You're glad because the way this conversation is going, it may not end well.

Karen looks at you dumbfounded. Charlene keeps trying to say something, but all she does is open and close her mouth.

"If this is how you treat your friends, I think I'd rather be somewhere else," Karen finally says.

She packs up her project and tells Charlene to follow her. Charlene does and they leave you, Craig, and C. J. motionless in the middle of the living room.

Just then your mom comes into the kitchen, interrupting your standoff.

"You kids want a hand?" she asks.

"We gotta get going," C. J. says. He pulls Craig by the arm and leads him out the front door.

You stare at that door for a long time. In one night you lost a lifetime of friends. It happened so fast.

You're not at all surprised when the grades are returned and you get a B. Craig flunks because Mr. Mac busted him on the black-market project. You laugh spitefully when you hear of it, but you sure don't feel good inside.

The End.

"Man, I can't believe you were that close to cheating," C. J. says.

Craig nods his head and looks at you again. "I'm sorry I gave you such a hard time outside the school earlier today," he confesses.

"I forgive you," you say, and you mean it. "Just don't let it happen again!" Your smile tells him everything's cool.

Craig looks around at the crumpled papers lying on the floor around your feet. "Hey, do you guys mind helping me figure out this project?" he asks.

Charlene kicks a paper ball toward the kitchen in frustration. "I need help, too," she says.

"We just need to think outside the box," suggests Karen. "Maybe we can find a topic that fits our personalities."

"Think?" complains C. J. "I hate thinking."

From the looks of things, everyone is thinking hard. C. J.'s eyes are scrunched shut. Karen keeps writing things down and then scribbling them out. Craig stares at the water spot on your ceiling. Charlene un-crumples and then re-crumples the papers that litter the floor.

"Hey, I wonder how many other dimwits pay for homework?" asks C. J., interrupting their unproductive silence.

"Who are you calling a dimwit?" demands Craig.

Great. Now everyone is off track. You know you won't come up with any ideas this way.

"Let's stay focused," you suggest. "We should each be able to figure out something." You remember your mom's promise if you ace this project. The stakes are high.

Within the next hour everyone has figured out a project—everyone except you.

"I'm starving," says C. J. "Can I make myself a sandwich?"

"Sure," you answer absentmindedly. You hear him pulling out items from the fridge.

"Pastrami?" C. J. says while unwrapping the deli packaging as if it might explode any minute. "Never heard of it. Is it good?"

"It's great!" Your mouth starts watering just thinking about it.

"It looks nasty," Charlene says. Charlene wouldn't eat it. She hates everything.

"I'll bet if you tasted it, you'd love it!" your mom says, walking in from the living room.

Suddenly an idea hatches in your brain—an eatable science project!

"I'm going to find out what is the favorite lunch meat at our school. Then I'm going to prove that when tasted, pastrami becomes the top choice," you say with great pride. What a genius idea! In fact it's the most original science project idea you've ever heard and *you* are the one who thought of it!

Five Alive just stares at you. Silent. With their mouths hanging open. Maybe it's too weird.

If you go ahead and pursue your Pastrami Project, go to page 38.

If you go back to the drawing board, go to page 40.

Michelle is sitting two rows ahead of you on the bus. She speaks just loud enough so you can hear her. She's not at all put off by Craig's earlier comment.

"Pastrami is the most disgusting lunch meat. No one eats it anymore. In fact, if you did, you'd probably puke right on the spot," Michelle says to anyone who will listen.

Everyone on the bus nods in agreement. In one fell swoop Michelle ruins your chance to survey fifty kids. This could be more serious than you thought.

"Hey, geek girl," Craig starts. "I puke every time I see you!"

Things are beginning to turn vicious.

If you tell Craig to leave her alone, go to page 42.

If you say nothing and ignore the jokes, go to page 44.

If you join in the jokes, go to page 45.

On Monday, the day everyone is supposed to present their science project ideas, Five Alive is actually excited. This is the first time you are *all* prepared. Mr. Mac will be shocked and hopefully impressed.

By the time it is your turn, it has become obvious that Five Alive has turned over a new leaf and everyone in your class notices. There's a lot of whispering going on, but that could be due to your increased *cool* status.

"I'm doing a Pastrami Project," you say. "I want to prove how delicious this sandwich meat is."

"Pastrami Project?" Mr. Mac asks. "Um, you're going to have to survey the entire student body to do what you say you want to do. Are you aware of that?"

To be honest, you hadn't thought the whole thing through yet, but you notice that right in the front row is Michelle—and she's smiling like a cat that just caught a bird. Why is it that you feel like the bird?

"I'm prepared," you lie. "No problem. In fact I will complete this project ahead of schedule." Why did you say that? There are a thousand kids in your middle school. There's no way to finish early!

"Then I will finish before you," Michelle says with complete confidence as you pass her desk to sit down. Michelle is the smartest kid in the class, probably in the entire sixth grade.

"Dream on, Michelle," says Craig. "You couldn't finish first if your life depended on it."

You know that Craig is just sticking up for you, but he was a little hard on Michelle. He's been teasing her since third grade and it doesn't seem like he has any intention of stopping now.

You really want to do well on this project, not just because your mom will pay you a handsome sum for doing so, but also because it would be nice to be on top just this once. No one, not even Michelle, will get in your way of getting the best grade on this project.

"She'll pay for trying to intimidate you," Craig says as you sit together on the bus. "It's time Michelle learned a lesson in humility."

Go to page 37.

Charlene sits with Craig and shows him her project so far. Craig starts nodding his head up and down with excitement.

"I get it. I get it. That's really cool, Charlene," he says. "Now I just need to come up with a great idea, too."

"We'll help you," Karen says. "Isn't that what friends are for?"

"I could use some help," you say. "Anyone want to help me figure out this pastrami survey?"

"You already know what your project is about," Charlene says. "Craig needs our help right now."

The girls encircle Craig like mother hens and they are deep in conversation. Craig is writing down furiously everything they say.

You look at the slices of pastrami your mom gave you as inspiration for your project. The slightly marbled, reddish meat that normally makes your mouth water has lost its appeal.

"Hey, you done with that?" C. J. asks pointing to your inspiration.

"Yeah, I guess I am," you say.

C. J. proceeds to gobble the pastrami and, with a full mouth, says, "You're right. This is the best lunchmeat I've ever tasted!"

You don't respond to C. J. because you're still watching Craig and the girls work on his project. He doesn't deserve this help. Why was it so easy for them to forgive him?

If you want to forgive Craig, go to page 86.
If you can't shake the bitterness, go to page 87.

"Chill, Craig," you say. "It's not worth it."

"She had it coming," he insists.

Michelle watches you and Craig.

"If she wants a competition, she's got one," you say. "Doesn't bother me in the least."

Craig looks out the window and pouts. You've ruined his fun. Craig is your friend and has been for eons, but sometimes his behavior borders on bullying. That part has always made you a little uncomfortable.

As everyone unloads at the bus stop you see Terry walking away from the stop. Terry has been invisible lately. It doesn't really matter at this point. You are so psyched about your science project. Wait until Terry and the others find out that yours is the best.

Five Alive meet at your house for the fifth straight night to work on projects. Everyone seems to know what to do. You haven't given much time or attention to anyone else's project, being so focused on your own. It feels good to be focused.

"One more piece," Charlene announces.

"Of what?" asks Karen.

"I just have to come up with an awesome way to do my presentation and then I'll be finished!" Charlene is absolutely beaming. You've never seen her so excited about anything that has anything to do with schoolwork before. She turns to you. "Listen, you took drama," she continues. "Can you help me write a monologue for my presentation?"

If you help Charlene, she could easily finish ahead of you, or, worse, get a better grade. That wasn't the plan.

If you help her, go to page 46.

If you don't help her, go to page 48.

Once off the bus, the teasing continues. Michelle walks ahead of Five Alive with two of her friends. You know she can hear Craig making fun of how she walks, how she talks, and even how she ignores him.

Karen and Charlene are giggling uncontrollably. You follow along quietly, wishing they'd all just stop. But they don't. Maybe it's no big deal. Maybe Michelle does deserve to be taken down a peg or two. After all, it is all kind of funny. You smile. Then your smile turns into laughter. Before you know it you lean over to Karen and Charlene and out comes your own opinion of what Michelle's hair looks like!

Michelle stops suddenly in the middle of the sidewalk. She turns around to face her tormentors. This is it. You suspect she is about to blast your friends for giving her such a hard time. You know they probably deserve it.

But when Michelle turns around her eyes fill with tears. She opens her mouth to speak, but nothing comes out. She turns then and runs into her house, slamming the door behind her.

"I don't think she likes what I said," you say to your friends.

Charlene bursts out laughing.

If you feel bad for Michelle, go to page 73.

If you like it that Charlene thinks you're funny, go to page 75.

"She's not geek girl," you whisper to Karen. "She's ghoul girl!"

Your friends roar with laughter.

This is the first time you've ever actually had something clever to say. You've always wanted to be more like Craig and Charlene, who are always witty.

The bus stops and you watch Michelle get up to leave. She turns to pick up her backpack and that's when you see it. Her eyes are red. She's been crying. No one else seems to have noticed. You and Five Alive follow a short distance behind Michelle.

If you feel bad for her, go to page 73.

If you like the attention you got for your wit, go to page 75.

"It's easy," you say. "Monologues are kind of like speeches, but they tend to have more of a personal touch to them."

"Can you help me write one?" Charlene asks her eyes big and pleading.

"I've got a lot on my plate trying to finish my own project," you say. "Let me think about it and get back to you tomorrow, okay?"

You are not as far ahead in your project as Charlene is. That surprises you. You've been working really hard, but obviously Charlene has been working even harder. You're torn. Being a good friend could easily cost you this competition.

That night you do something you haven't done in a while. You pray. God hasn't played a real big part in this whole scenario. You think you've done pretty well all on your own. You hesitate in your prayer, feeling like you should have included him sooner than this.

God, I know I've been trying to do this project on my own without your help. I'm sorry for not including you sooner. I thought I had it covered. I was wrong. I want to help Charlene, but I can't help thinking how it may affect my own chances. Help me to help my friend even if it means giving up something I want for myself. I've been selfish. I want both—to help my friend and to do well on my project. Please help me do what I need to do! Amen.

You actually sleep well that night, and the next morning you are sure you can help Charlene. It's Saturday, so you have all day to work with her on her monologue if you need to. Charlene is so happy, and after only an hour she completely understands how to write the monologue herself. You have the rest of the day to work on your own project.

If you start to work on your own project, go to page 50.

If you keep helping Charlene, go to page 53.

"I have no idea, Charlene," you say without looking at her. "I guess you're on your own with this one."

This competition is too important to you to blow it by letting even one of your friends get the advantage over you.

"No problem. I'll ask someone else," she says. She doesn't seem bothered by the fact that you won't help her.

Two days later as Five Alive meets again to work on projects, Charlene is beaming.

"What's up with you?" asks Craig.

"I'm done! I'm really done," she says.

You can't believe your ears! How can she be done? You're not even near done.

"Cool!" says Karen. "Hey, how did you figure out how to do your presentation anyway?"

"I asked Michelle," Charlene says. "She's pretty smart, you know."

Michelle? Why would Michelle help Charlene? And then it hits you. Michelle would do anything at this point to beat you, even if it meant helping one of your friends.

"Well, it looks like you'll turn in your project on time," you say, trying not to let Charlene hear your disappointment.

"I already did." Charlene is practically floating with pride, but she doesn't seem to be aware of your hard feelings toward her.

Two weeks later grades for the science projects are returned. You get a B-. Michelle and Charlene get As, plus bonus points for turning in their projects early.

The End.

You have just a few days left to finish your project. You accept the fact that you will not finish early. At this point you'll settle for finishing on time! Getting people to fill out a short survey on their favorite lunchmeat took more time than you expected. Then offering a taste test took even longer. Thank goodness your mom bought the pastrami and helped you make little bite-sized sandwiches. At first kids wouldn't taste it. They weren't used to red, marbled sandwich meat with seasoned pepper around the edges. But you were right! They liked it. They really liked it!

You ignored Michelle's peacock-like parade of her own project turned in two days before the deadline. She worked hard. She deserves a good grade. It seems like most everyone else waited until the last minute as well. Craig is really nervous about his project.

"Maybe I should have just handed in the project I bought," he says.

"No way!" you say in horror. "Be proud that you did your project yourself. We're proud of you."

All of Five Alive nod in agreement. In fact they're all pretty proud of themselves, too. This is the first time all of you turned in anything on time. Mr. Mac even commented on it.

Two weeks later you expect to find out your grade, but it doesn't come. Mr. Mac says he's discovered a problem and grades will be delayed. You squirm in your seat even though you have no reason to worry.

"What do you think the problem is?" asks Karen.

"Maybe Mr. Mac doesn't believe we did our own projects," Craig says. "After all, we've never all turned them in before."

"Mr. Mac wouldn't suspect us of anything," you say. "He helped us when we needed it, didn't he? It must be something else."

"Or *someone* else," Karen says. "I'd hate to be that someone."

Finally Mr. Mac hands back the projects. Everyone except Terry, Billy, and a couple other kids find out their grade. They are so busted! You feel no sympathy for Terry.

Walking out of class, Craig runs up to you.

"I am so glad I threw that black-market project away," he says.

"Me, too," you say. You're also really glad you never gave in to that temptation yourself.

"Thanks," Craig says. He stands there frozen. You put out your hand to make it easier on him.

"You're welcome. What are friends for?"

Charlene saves a seat for you on the bus.

"I didn't want to open mine until we were all together," she says. She slowly opens her project envelope and silently reads her grade. She looks up at you and mouths 'A.'

Five Alive explode with cheering and laughter. Everyone on the bus turns to see about the commotion. The bus driver yells at you to quiet down, but it makes you laugh all the more. Everyone swaps projects and the verdict is in. Five Alive is cool—way cool! All of you get As. But the best and most surprising part is that you and Charlene get bonus points on top of it all. *For quality work and originality* is handwritten on both your projects.

The End.

"I really think a dramatic monologue is the best choice for your presentation," you tell Charlene.

"You mean something like 'Four score and seven years ago …'?" Charlene mimics President Lincoln's address.

"I hope yours will be more interesting than that!" you say. The two of you burst out laughing. Helping Charlene might actually be fun!

Two hours later Charlene has a real start on her monologue.

"I can take it from here," she says. "Thanks for showing me how to do this."

"No problem!" you say, but you're only half listening to Charlene because suddenly your brain is flooded with great ideas for your own project. It's like a light went on to show you all the ideas that were just lurking there in the dark.

"I gotta go," you tell her. "I hope you do great on your project."

Before Charlene can answer, you're out the door and on your way home to put the finishing touches on your own project.

Two weeks later Mr. Mac hands out the project grades. You get an A with bonus points for creativity. What a cool feeling! You've never done this well before. And it wasn't that hard, either.

If you want to keep up the good work with your friends, go to page 88.
If you love being the best, go to page 89.

"You're crazy, Terry. I know I'd get caught somehow. Besides," you begin, feeling a little embarrassed, "I guess I'd rather not cheat."

Terry shrugs. "Fine by me."

"Okay," you say. "Well, I'll see you around." You turn to walk away."Think about what I said," Terry calls just before disappearing around the corner. "Do it my way and we'd have more time to play ball together." Terry is definitely full of surprises— you just didn't expect cheating to be one of them.

"Hey, hon," Mom calls to you as you enter the house. You thought you were quiet enough that she wouldn't hear you. "Tonight's the night!"

You play dumb. "For what?"

"To get you started on your best science project ever, silly!"

If you tell her the truth, go to page 55.

If you tell her you don't need any help, go to page 58.

"Mom, I don't think we can work on my project tonight," you begin. You're ready to spill your guts. You just pray she doesn't get too mad.

"Sure we can. It's not that late," your mom says while warming up some dinner for you.

"You don't understand, Mom. I didn't go see Mr. Mac today. I still have no clue how to do this project." There, you said it.

Your mom continues to set your place at the table, takes the food from the microwave, and starts to wash the dishes—all without saying a word. You sit down at the table and pick at your food. You feel like a total jerk. Then you remember that your mom cancelled plans she had that night just to work with you on your project. You feel even worse.

"I'm sorry, Mom. I'm really sorry," you say.

She takes a deep breath and then smiles at you.

"It doesn't matter. I'll bet we can figure it out for ourselves."

"I don't know. I don't even have an idea of what it should be about," you say. You're amazed that your mom is still willing to help you.

"How about we give it a try?" she says.

"I'm willing if you are," you say. Just then your appetite returns and you almost inhale your food. You didn't know you were that hungry.

It's ten o'clock at night and the living room floor is littered with papers. Your mom is sitting on the floor looking exhausted.

"This isn't working," you say. "I don't know if I'm supposed to do an experiment or create some sort of display."

"Let's go online and look for some ideas," your mom suggests.

"We did that two hours ago," you say and yawn so wide your jaw cracks.

"Okay, let's try reading through some of my old textbooks."

You are too tired and too frustrated to care anymore about this project. You just want to go to bed.

If you ask your mom if she'll please help another night, go to page 60.

If you yell at your mom, go to page 62.

"No problem, Mom," you say. "I've got it under control."

"Mr. Mac must have explained it then," she says.

"Not really," you say, careful not to actually lie to her. "A friend helped me."

"Well, I set the whole night aside just for you. I'll help you get started," Mom says and then starts to clear the dining room table.

"No," you say a little more alarmed than you intended. "I don't need your help. I can do it myself."

Your mom gives you the I-know-there's-more-to-this look. "Okay. If you say so," she says without pushing you for an answer.

The next couple of weeks are the most frustrating you've ever experienced. You know there's no way you'll get a good enough grade to earn that $25. You wonder what's the point of even trying.

The night before the project is due you consider asking your mom to finally help you. Unfortunately she has to work late and won't be home in time to offer any help. You are completely on your own—just as you told her you wanted to be.

When grades are returned on the projects, you're surprised that you got a C. You expected worse than that.

The End.

"Mom, how about we look at this again tomorrow," you suggest.

Your mom sighs. "Maybe you're right," she says. "We could both use some sleep. Make sure that you're around all day tomorrow, though, so we can figure this out before Monday."

You are so glad you decided not to take Terry up on the black-market homework offer. As you drift off to sleep you feel peaceful and encouraged that all will be well.

The next morning your mom has cooked pancakes and is just getting off the phone when you walk downstairs.

"Eat up, we've got a big day ahead of us." Your mom is way too perky in the morning.

"Who were you talking to?" you ask, still in a it's-way-too-early-for-any-civilized-person-to-be-up mood.

"I called your science teacher," she said quite proud of herself.

"You what?" you say in horror. She called your teacher on a Sunday?

"I remember he gave us his home phone number at Open House for emergencies. This certainly qualifies."

For just a moment you are mortified that your mom actually called your teacher. Especially since you didn't show up yesterday for the help session as promised.

"What did he say?" you ask and then wince as if you are waiting for some very bad news.

"He explained it all. I understand completely now," your mom says. "Are you ready to get started?"

"In a minute," you say with a mouthful of blueberry-syrup-covered pancakes.

"Well, hurry up so I can clear this table before your friends get here," she says.

You choke on your pancakes. "What? Why?"

"I suspected that you were probably not the only one of your friends who didn't know what he was doing. Well, except for Karen. She is always on top of her studies," she says. "I called them all, and they'll be here soon."

Go to page 38.

"Mom, forget it! I just want to go to bed," you say with obvious annoyance.

"I know it's been awhile since I've been in school, but I know I can help you," she says and frantically sorts through all the papers on the dining room table.

"No, you can't. You don't have a clue how to help me. I'm going to bed," you say and storm out of the room and slam your bedroom door.

A few minutes later there is a soft rap at your bedroom door.

"May I come in?" your mom asks.

"Do what you want. It's your house," you say. Your mood hasn't improved.

"Yes," she says, "it is."

And you know what she means.

"I made you something to eat," she says and puts a plate and a glass of milk on your nightstand. "Pastrami, mustard, and cheese."

Pastrami. Your favorite, but right now it only reminds you of your problem. You don't even touch it.

"I'm sorry I don't understand your project enough to help you," she says. "I know you're frustrated."

"That's for sure," you say, softening a little—could be hunger, could be the way your mom looks at you.

"I love you, sweetie, and I'm always here if you need me," she says and moves toward the door.

At that moment you feel tons better. It doesn't solve your problem, but you want things to be right between you and your mom. You pick up the pastrami sandwich and take a luscious bite.

"And by the way," she says, "you're grounded for a week for the way you talked to me earlier. Sleep well."

If you are sorry, go to page 60.

If you are mad, go to page 77.

"You know what? I've changed my mind," you say. "I don't need your services after all." Suddenly you feel lighter, more peaceful.

"You wasted my time!" he says. "I'll let Terry know how lame you are."

You watch Billy ride away and wonder what Terry will think of you now.

If you have a plan for Five Alive, go to page 84.

If you have a plan for you, go to page 85.

"I'll get you the money. Don't worry," you say. "How much for a grade A science project?"

"Ten bucks cash," he says. "By Friday or the deal is off."

You attempt to shake hands with Billy, but he turns away and starts to walk to the bike rack. As he rides away, he calls over his shoulder at you, "Nice doin' business with you."

That night you bum money off Five Alive. You tell them it's to buy your mom a present. They all like your mom, so they each chip in a few bucks. You raid your penny bank and come up with the rest. On Friday you make the trade with Billy. Why is it you don't feel relieved?

All your friends are working hard on their science projects. You are so glad to have these friends: Charlene, the athlete. Karen, the kindhearted. C. J. the goof. Craig the comic. But now they're all too busy to even play ball with you. Even C. J. is taking his project seriously. That's a first! When your mom asks you how your project is going, you tell her you've got it all under control.

Two weeks later Mr. Mac returns their science projects to everyone except you, Billy, and Terry. You squirm in your seat because you know you've been busted. Five Alive watch you as you're marched down to the principal's office. They are in shock that you would cheat.

When you arrive at the principal's office, Billy and Terry are joking around and think the whole thing is stupid. You are horrified to see your mom already sitting inside the principal's office. You know she had to leave work to be there.

After being grounded for six weeks you look for your friends, but they avoid you.

"We don't know who you are anymore," Karen says.

Your mom doesn't seem to trust you anymore, either. Staying alone in your room every day is a very lonely existence. And, to top it all off, you flunked science.

The End.

You know you should apologize, but you're not sure if you can make yourself do it. You cry out to God from your bed.

Lord, I really messed things up today. I got so angry. Craig made a bad decision, but I shouldn't have called him names. Forgive me for making an even bigger mistake out of being angry. Help me to say sorry to Craig. And please help him to forgive me. Amen. Oh, also help him not to use that project he bought.

The next morning Craig is waiting for you at the bus stop as usual. You didn't expect him to even talk to you, but he does.

"What's up?" he says.

"I was up, that's for sure," you begin. He glances at you. You nod and continue. "I couldn't sleep last night, Craig. I'm really sorry for jumping down your throat like that yesterday."

Craig looks down at the crack in the sidewalk and straddles it with his feet. He says nothing.

"Still pals?" you ask, although you know he has every right not to ever talk to you again.

"Pals," Craig says.

That night Five Alive meet at your house to work on science projects and Craig comes. He works on his project, which leads you to think he decided not to use the black-market homework from Billy. You don't say anything about it. You're just happy to have your friend back.

Your final grade on the project isn't as good as you hoped for, but you know you were sort of distracted because of the rift between you and Craig. You think you could have done better, but the B+ you got was probably generous of Mr. Mac.

The End.

That night you can't sleep. You keep thinking about your argument with Craig. You've known each other since kindergarten! Craig can be stubborn and even difficult at times, but today he crossed the line.

The next morning at the bus stop Craig starts right away finding ways to give you a hard time. You're not used to his biting wit coming your way. He usually reserves this for his worst enemies. Is that what you are now?

A few times Karen, Charlene, and C. J. try to lighten the mood. But even C. J.'s goofy obsession with snack food doesn't make you laugh.

You and Craig can't find a way to be around each other, and eventually Five Alive falls apart. You work on your projects on your own. You don't even care at this point.

You're not surprised at the grade you receive: C+.

The End.

You are quiet for a moment. You have never known Karen to be unfair to you.

"Okay," you say reluctantly. "Tell me what you're thinking."

"It's just that I've just never seen you that angry," Karen says. "Especially to one of your best friends."

"But he did something really wrong."

"Yeah, but you should help him to make it right, not walk away from the friendship."

You nod your head.

"Are you going to make it right between the two of you?" she asks.

You look at C. J. and Charlene. They both nod their heads in agreement with Karen.

"Okay. I'll talk to him," you say.

"I'm glad," Karen says. "You really got me worried yesterday."

"How?"

"I started to think that if you talked about Craig the way you did, do you ever talk about me or the rest of the gang that way?" Karen doesn't even look at you. "I mean, I do stupid things all the time. Do you get that mad at me?" Her voice cracks, and you can tell she's close to tears.

This has gotten blown out of proportion. Where did this all start? Craig was the one who bought the black-market homework. Terry was the one who led him down that path. Why is it that it all feels like your fault?

You want things to be normal again. But you wonder why you're the one who has to make it happen. "Listen," you say. "I'm sorry, okay?"

"Prove it," says Charlene. She whips out her cell phone. "I'm calling Craig."

"Wait!" you say.

"Wait? Why?" demands Charlene.

If you agree to talk to Craig, go to page 26.
If you chicken out, go to page 28.

"Michelle, wait!" you yell and run to her front door.

Five Alive stand on the sidewalk, looking puzzled.

You ring the doorbell and take a step back from the door. It doesn't hurt to be safe.

"May I help you?" Michelle's mom answers the door.

"Umm, yes. Can I talk to Michelle?" Michelle's mom eyes you suspiciously. You can tell Michelle has already told her about your torments. You look desperately into her eyes as if pleading for one more chance.

"I'll get her for you," she says. She must have believed you. "But I wouldn't expect a smile from her if I were you."

A moment later Michelle is at the door, but sort of hiding behind it. You can tell she's been crying.

"Michelle, I'm really sorry for ganging up on you like that," you say. "It was stupid."

"You're right about that," she says, but not very bravely.

"It won't happen again. I promise," you say.

"Sure it won't," she says. She obviously doesn't believe you, but who could blame her?

The door slams in your face and you stand there a minute longer.

Go to page 79.

What a rush! It feels great that people laugh at your jokes. You never thought of yourself as funny, but today is the start of a brand new image for you.

You know you helped make Michelle cry, but she deserves a little grief now and then. Maybe she won't be so stuck-up in the future.

You start cracking more jokes over the next couple weeks. Your jokes are getting good, and you feel like you need an audience beyond Five Alive. You're kind of surprised at how easy it is to be funny, as long as there is someone nearby with something embarrassing to point out. You begin talking extra loud on the bus and at the lunch table.

When it's time to turn in your science project, you know yours is pretty shabby. The last week you didn't work on it at all; you were too busy hanging out with anyone who would listen to your jokes. The rest of your gang worked on theirs.

The day comes when the grades are handed out for the projects. You tease each person who walks to the front to get their project—even Karen and Charlene. The class is abuzz with muffled giggles. You're a riot!

Finally it's your turn. You grab the paper right out of Mr. Mac's hands and actually skip back to your seat. The C- you got doesn't even faze you. You're famous! Everyone knows you for your humor, not your grades.

As the weeks slip by, you notice that your friends don't include you anymore. You try not to care. "It's lonely at the top," you say with a laugh to anyone who will listen.

The End.

Your mom closes the door and leaves you to your sandwich and your thoughts. You've lost your appetite and lie in bed trying to decide who to blame for this mess. You think your mom was too hard on you. Grounded for a week! You fall asleep finally, still angry.

You stick to what you told your mom and don't ask for any help on your project. You turn it in knowing that it is not near what you wanted it to be. When you get your grade back two weeks later, you're not surprised that you got a C+ on it.

The End.

After Five Alive leave that night, you uncrumple Craig's black market project you rescued from the trash earlier. You are stunned! It's only a B project! Why would Craig pay money for a B?

You want an A on this project, and you're willing to do whatever it takes to get one.

If you keep working hard, go to page 38.

If you find Billy to buy a project, go to page 19.

You walk back to your friends, who stare at you.

"Ah, leave me alone," you say. "We were pretty rotten to her."

Charlene shrugs. "Yeah, I guess we were." She punches you gently on the shoulder. "I wish I had said sorry to her, too."

The rest of the group nods and you begin moving down the sidewalk again.

Five Alive meet at your house for the fifth straight night to work on projects. Everyone seems to know what to do. You haven't given much time or attention to anyone else's project, being so focused on your own. It feels good to be focused.

"One more piece," Charlene announces.

"Of what?" asks Karen.

"I just have to come up with an awesome way to do my presentation and then I'll be finished!" Charlene is absolutely beaming. You've never seen her so excited about anything that has anything to do with schoolwork before. She turns to you. "Listen, you took drama," she continues. "Can you help me write a monologue for my presentation?"

If you help Charlene, she could easily finish ahead of you, or, worse, get a better grade. That wasn't the plan.

If you help her, go to page 46.

If you don't help her, go to page 48.

He shakes his head and smiles. "I guess the velocity of that ball surprised me a bit."

"Thanks, Mr. Mac—for everything," you say.

"That's what I'm here for. I'm here every Saturday for a couple of hours if you need me."

Somehow you feel lighter, more at ease as you leave the school. It feels good to not feel lost in science. This could be a brand new start to the rest of the school year.

"Hey, did you serve your sentence?" a voice says from behind you.

"Craig. I didn't see you there," you say feeling both a little surprised and a little annoyed at the same time.

"While you were in there wasting your time with Mr. Mac the science maniac, I made some real progress."

He hands you about six or seven well-worn papers.

"I'm set for the rest of the week in every subject," he says with pride.

"You bought these?" you ask.

"Yeah. Your friend Terry set me up. I have better things to do with my time than homework."

You thrust the papers back into his hands and start to walk away.

"Hey, what's wrong with you?" Craig asks.

"I was just going to ask you the same question," you say, turning toward him.

"I thought you were smart. I guess I was wrong."

"Who are you—the homework police?" Craig starts laughing.

If you offer to help Craig with his homework, go to page 21.

If you get mad at him, go to page 22.

That night, the rest of Five Alive show up at your house to work on science projects. "Great!" your mom says. "The more of us, the better. We'll get this figured out."

You're glad your friends like your mom, and it is pretty cool to see them actually working, but you've got your mind on something else. You eye the clock, thinking Craig will come to his senses and show up. The minutes tick away and turn into hours.

"Okay, kids," your mom finally says. "I've got some work to do. Let me know if you need any more help." She disappears into the living room.

"What's with you?" Charlene asks you as soon as your mom is gone.

"Got any more chips?" C. J. asks while rummaging through the kitchen.

"In the pantry," you tell him.

Now Charlene is in your face.

"You made us all come here to work on our science projects, but you've been someplace else all night."

"No, I haven't," you say, not looking at Charlene. You look at the phone, willing it to ring.

"Then what do you call this?" Charlene holds up your paper, your empty paper. "The rest of us have a million ideas. You have nothing!"

"Yeah, and what do you call this?" C. J. now stands in the living room with an empty bag of chips.

You grab the bag from C. J. and crumple it before tossing it into the trash.

"Hey, there were crumbs in there!"

"Forget it," you say.

For five solid minutes it is quiet. Not even C. J.'s crunching of remnant chips from the bottom of the nachos bag can be heard.

"Okay, spit it out," Karen finally says. "We know something's wrong."

You know your friends will listen to whatever you have to say. You're just not sure you want to say it while you're so mad. If you blurt out the news tonight, you don't know if you'll be able to say anything good about Craig at all.

If you wait for a better time to talk, go to page 23.

If you tell your friends what Craig has done, go to page 25.

You gather your friends together. "I have an amazing plan," you say.

"What?" groans Craig. "Don't tell me we're going to have Operation Terry to get the two of you together."

"No way," you say. "I'm not interested in Terry anymore." It feels good to know this is true. "No. I think it's about time Five Alive turns over a new leaf."

"What do you mean?" asks Karen.

"Let's work together to see if we can all get As on our science projects."

"What's wrong with getting Cs?" C. J. says. "Cs stand for *cool*, don't they?"

"Technically, Cs mean average," Karen says. "Personally, I think that cool should be way above average."

"Then maybe it's time we show what we're made of," you say. You're so excited at the prospect of being cool *and* getting great grades. What a concept!

"I'm in," Karen says and puts her hand up for a high five. "Who's with me?"

The five of you slap it high and down low.

Go to page 38.

"Who needs Terry?" you say to yourself. "I can get an A without cheating."

You sit at your desk in your bedroom that night, determined to figure out how to have the best science project in the school. You think about calling Five Alive to brainstorm together; but you stop yourself when you realize that if you do, they'll probably get good grades, too. And you want the glory for yourself, just this once. You want to show Terry.

As hard as you try, you can't come up with a good idea for your project. You finally turn in a boring essay on dinosaurs. You get a B-.

The End.

You try to work on your own project, but you can't help feeling jealous. You silently ask God to help you not be so bitter. After all, Jesus has forgiven you for a whole lot of stuff.

After a few minutes you feel better. You're even glad that Craig is back.

Go to page 38.

You get nothing done that night, and you're too mad at your friends to ask them to help you later.

You get sick of the science project and work very little on it. You get a C+.

The End.

Five Alive comes to your house to celebrate your good work. Your mom orders a bunch of pizzas and lets you blast your music.

"Oh, yeah!" you say to your friends enthusiastically. "We've got to keep this up."

Your friends all agree, and you decide that life is pretty good.

The End.

You turn into the perfect student. You spend all your time perfecting your homework and projects. Your goal is to get straight As for the rest of the school year.

At the end-of-the-year awards ceremony, you are disappointed not to see your friends there to cheer you on. You are getting three awards, including top honor student. You haven't spent any time with Five Alive, and your victory is hollow. You've never been so lonely in your life.

The End.

Life Issue: **I want to do my best without hurting others.**

Spiritual Building Block: **Wisdom**

Do the following activities to help not getting so caught up in yourself that you stop helping others:

Talk About It:

As Christians, we depend on one another for encouragement and advice. God does not expect us to walk alone.

Find someone outside of your group of friends who you admire for making the right decisions—a parent, a teacher, a minister, or a coach. Look for someone who will not be affected by your decision so they can give you neutral advice.

Explain your situation and what choices you think you have, along with any details that are influencing your decision.

Ask what she would do if she were in your shoes. Sometimes just saying your problem out loud helps you find the answer. Hearing someone else's take on your situation can show you something you may not have thought of before.

Faith Builder
Ages 9 and up
Wisdom

Life Issue: **I want to do my best without hurting others.**

Spiritual Building Block: **Wisdom**

Do the following activities to help not getting so caught up in yourself that you stop helping others:

Think About It:

When you're faced with making a decision that could impact you and someone you care about, don't decide on the spot.

Take a bike ride or a walk or just shut yourself in your room for a while.

Think through how your different actions in the situation could affect you and others. Make a list of pros and cons for each of the choices that face you. Remember the Golden Rule.

Consider how you would want others to react in this same situation if it affected you. Remember the phrase WWJD (What would Jesus do?). Think about that.

Pray to God for guidance. If you turn to him he will help you know what a Christian should do.

Life Issue: **I want to do my best without hurting others.**

Spiritual Building Block: **Wisdom**

Do the following activities to help not getting so caught up in yourself that you stop helping others:

Try It:

After looking over which choice has more positive outcomes than negative ones, listening to a trusted confidant's advice, and searching in your heart for what you think Jesus would do, act upon your decision.

Help your friends even if it means taking time away from something you enjoy, walk away from a chance to lie or cheat to make yourself look better at someone else's expense, respect your parents' wishes about something even if they don't seem to understand.

Then pray to God for the courage to follow through with your choice.

You'll be amazed at how good you'll feel for doing the right thing!

Collect all the books
in the series!
God Allows U-Turns Youth

The reader becomes the main character in these stories about tight friendships, families, and the choices kids make. The choices the reader makes while going through the story determines the outcome. Will you figure out how to handle friendships and faith without messing up? Will you make good decisions and be the kind of friend others trust? Will you get caught up in you own world, or will you remember how your choices affect others? Even if you make the wrong choices, there's still good news—God allows u-turns!

$4.99 each   *(Can. $7.99)*
5 7/16 x 8   Paperback   96P

Get Real!
ISBN: 0-78143-974-4
Item #: 102867

Friend or Freak
ISBN: 0-78143-972-8
Item #: 102865

The
God Allows U-Turns Ministry

Along with the exciting children's books published by Cook Communications, we want to share with readers the entire scope of the powerful God Allows U-Turns ministry of hope and healing. The broad outreach of this ministry includes the book you now hold in your hands, as well as a series of true short-story anthologies called *God Allows U-Turns, True Stories of Hope and Healing*. Multiple volumes in the popular compilation series are now available at bookstores internationally.

Bible book covers, back packs, ball caps, greeting cards, calendars, and more all bear the recognizable U-Turns road sign logo. The "New Direction Tour" featuring speakers, music, and more is also in the planning stages with the first event premiering in 2004 in a major USA city to be announced. Additionally, a cable television interview talk show, hosted by Allison Bottke, will soon be coming to homes around the world called: God Allows U-Turns—Real People, Real Issues, Real Faith, featuring interviews with people who have made dramatic U-turns.

For updates on the expanding ministry visit the God Allows U-Turns web site at http://www.godallowsuturns.com or write to Allison Bottke at: P.O. Box 717, Faribault, MN 55021-0717.

God Allows U-Turns for Kids
Laughter and Love
Picnics and Peace
Jingles and Joy

God Allows U-Turns for Youth
Friend or Freak
Pastrami Project
Get Real!

The Word at Work Around the World

W̶hat would you do if you wanted to share God's love with children on the streets of your city? That's the dilemma David C. Cook faced in 1870's Chicago. His answer was to create literature that would capture children's hearts.

Out of those humble beginnings grew a worldwide ministry that has used literature to proclaim God's love and disciple generation after generation. Cook Communications Ministries is committed to personal discipleship—to helping people of all ages learn God's Word, embrace his salvation, walk in his ways, and minister in his name.

Faith Kidz, RiverOak, Honor, Life Journey, Victor, NextGen . . . every time you purchase a book produced by Cook Communications Ministries, you not only meet a vital personal need in your life or in the life of someone you love, but you're also a part of ministering to José in Colombia, Humberto in Chile, Gousa in India, or Lidiane in Brazil. You help make it possible for a pastor in China, a child in Peru, or a mother in West Africa to enjoy a life-changing book. And because you helped, children and adults around the world are learning God's Word and walking in his ways.

Thank you for your partnership in helping to disciple the world. May God bless you with the power of his Word in your life.

For more information about our international ministries, visit www.ccmi.org.